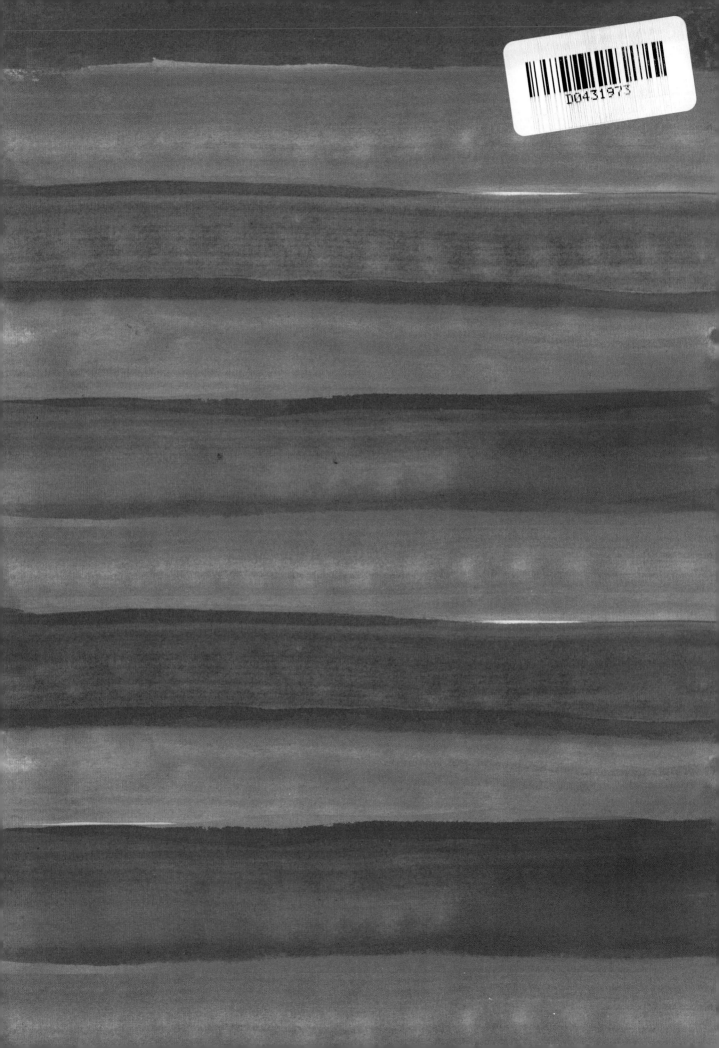

for Henry, Mary, and Weezie

Copyright © 2018 by Vern Kousky

All rights reserved. Published in the United States by Schwartz & Wade Books,

an imprint of Random House Children's Books, a division of Penguin Random House LLC, New York.

Schwartz & Wade Books and the colophon are trademarks of Penguin Random House LLC.

Visit us on the Web! rhcbooks.com

Educators and librarians, for a variety of teaching tools, visit us at RHTeachersLibrarians.com

Library of Congress Cataloging-in-Publication Data is available upon request.

ISBN 978-1-5247-6467-8 (hc)

ISBN 978-1-5247-6468-5 (lib. bdg.)

ISBN 978-1-5247-6469-2 (ebook)

The text of this book was hand-lettered in pencil.

The illustrations were rendered with pencil, pen, and watercolor and manipulated digitally.

MANUFACTURED IN CHINA

10 9 8 7 6 5 4 3 2 1

First Edition

HAROLD LOVES HIS
WOOLLY HAT

Vern Kousky

schwartz & wade books · new york

Harold loves to wear his woolly hat.

Even in the summertime.

He wears it when
he goes to school.

He wears it when
he goes to sleep.

Harold even wears his woolly hat
when he takes his monthly bath.

When Harold wears his woolly hat,
he knows he is a special bear —

different from all the other bears.

Then one day, a crow swoops
down and steals Harold's
woolly hat.

*Now I look just like all the other
bears,* thinks Harold. *How will
anyone know that I am a very
special bear?*

Harold has to win back his woolly hat.

He gathers up some wriggly worms
and says to the crow, "Let's trade!"

The crow swoops down

and takes the worms

and flies them to its nest.

"Now please give me back
my woolly hat," shouts Harold.

But the crow only replies,

CaCAW! CaCAW!!

So Harold tries to
make another trade.

"Here are
some tasty
blueberries
for you."

The crow swoops down

and takes the berries

and flies them to its nest.

"NOW PLEASE GIVE ME
BACK MY WOOLLY HAT!"

Again, the crow just replies,

CaCAW! CaCAW!

"What a greedy little crow," growls Harold. "I'll never win back my woolly hat."

Then he remembers his secret collection of shiny things.

"Here you go, you mean old crow. I've got the perfect trade for you."

The crow swoops down

and takes the things

and flies them to its nest.

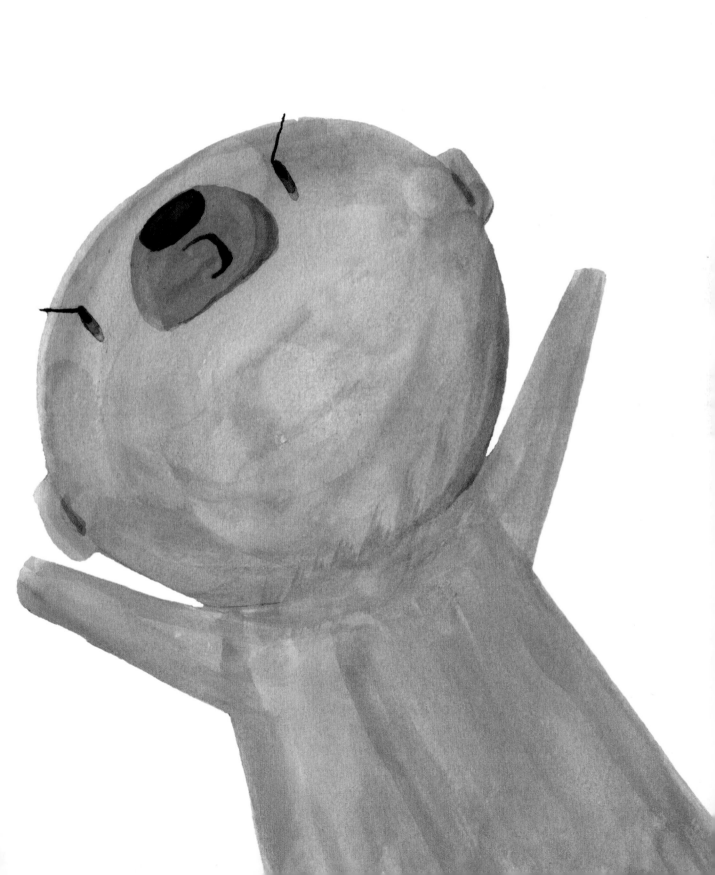

Once more, the crow only replies,

CaCAW! CaCAW!

There's just one thing
left for Harold to do.

He hides behind a
rock and waits
until the crow
flies away.

Then he sneaks over to the tree,

and sees...

climbs

up,

up,

up

to the

tippy-top,

three baby crows!

Harold tucks the crows in tight,
then quietly climbs down from the nest.

"Even without my woolly hat," he whispers,

"I am still a very special bear."

"A helpful bear named Harold."